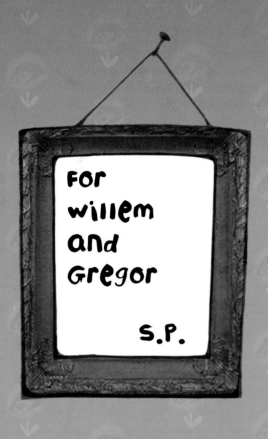

For
Willem
and
Gregor

S.P.

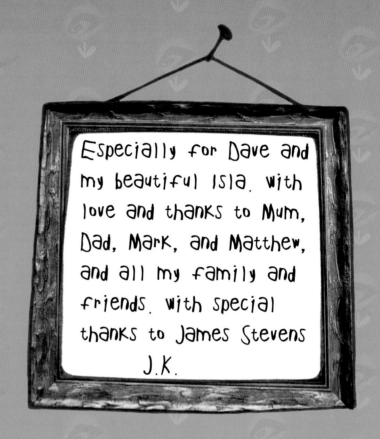

Especially for Dave and
my beautiful Isla. With
love and thanks to Mum,
Dad, Mark, and Matthew,
and all my family and
friends. With special
thanks to James Stevens

J.K.

Yours Truly, Louisa

Text copyright © 2009 by Simon Puttock

Illustrations copyright © 2009 by Jo Kiddie

Library of Congress Cataloging-in-Publication Data is available.

ISBN 978-0-06-136634-5 (trade bdg.)

1 2 3 4 5 6 7 8 9 10

❖

First American Edition, 2009

Originally published in Great Britain by HarperCollins Children's Books

Yours Truly, Louisa

by **Simon Puttock**

illustrated by
Jo Kiddie

HarperCollins*Publishers*

Louisa the pig was *not* pleased.
The farm was a *mess.*
"Something," said Louisa,
"must be done about this."

So she wrote a letter to Farmer Joe.

Dear Farmer Joe,

The farm is filthy. Please clean it up at once!

Yours truly,

Disgruntled!

Farmer Joe scratched his head. "Who could the letter be from?" he wondered. "Whoever it is has a point. I'll clean it up."

Farmer Joe swept the barn,

cleaned out the henhouse,

and tidied up the pigsty too.
"That," he said, "ought to do it."

But Louisa the pig was not impressed.
"Huh," she thought, and she wrote
another letter.

Dear Farmer Joe,
You have not done
enough. Please
do more.

Yours truly,

Disgruntled!

Farmer Joe WAS surprised. "Well," he said,
"I suppose I could give the barn a fresh coat of paint."
So the next morning, he got up bright and early
and painted the barn a beautiful shade of blue.
Then he painted the henhouse, the pigsty,
and his front door too.

"There we go,"
said Farmer Joe,
admiring his handiwork.

the farm

But Louisa the pig
did not agree, and she
wrote another letter.

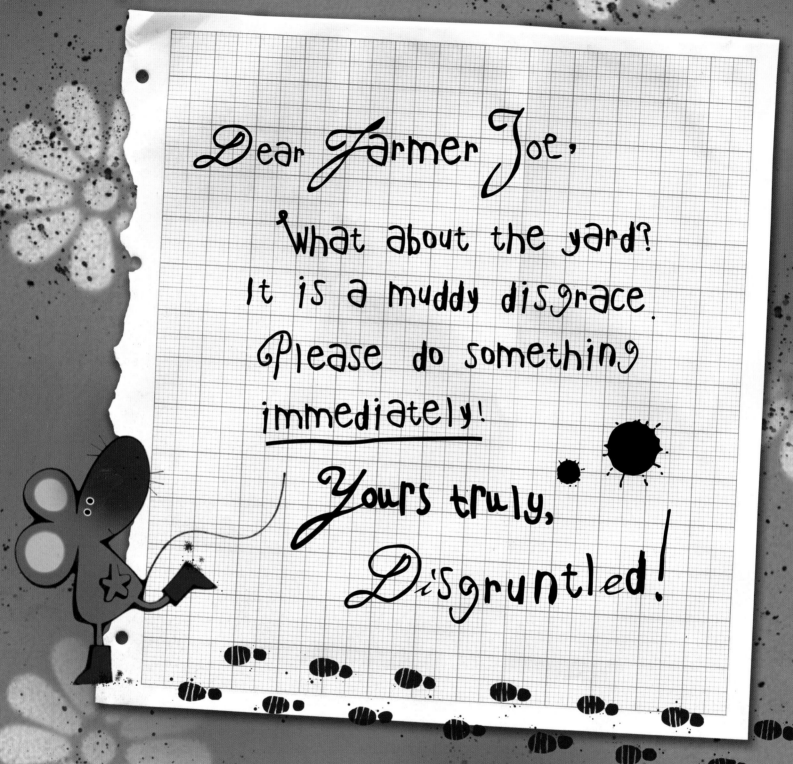

Dear Farmer Joe,
What about the yard?
It is a muddy disgrace.
Please do something
immediately!

Yours truly,
Disgruntled!

Farmer Joe was stumped.
"A barnyard's MADE for mud," he muttered.

"... but it does get all over.
I'll see what I can do."

The next morning, Farmer Joe
was up before the rooster.

- c · o · c · k · a · d · o · o · d · l · e · d · o · o

He got a great big
roller and rolled . . .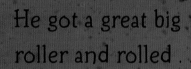

and rolled . . .

and rolled the barnyard until it shone like chocolate icing.

Louisa the pig just sniffed, "Mud is such a dreary color."

And she wrote another letter.

Dear Farmer Joe,
The farm is now tidy, but it is also very dull.
Please brighten it up. The sooner, the better.
Yours truly,
Disgruntled!

"Who can Disgruntled BE?" wondered Farmer Joe.
"But . . . a bit of color *would* cheer the place up."

So the next morning, before the sun had even begun to rise, Farmer Joe drove into town and shopped . . .

and shopped . . .

and shopped.

Then he took his shopping home and planted it.
The farmyard looked remarkable!
"And THAT," said Farmer Joe, "is THAT!"
But . . .

Louisa the pig quickly wrote another note.

Dear Farmer Joe,

A good effort, but I look around and what do I see? The fields could use a trim (turnips are such untidy vegetables) and there are cow pies everywhere. While you're at it, the sheep are in terrible need of haircuts.

Yours truly,

Disgruntled!

"Enough," shouted Farmer Joe, "is enough! This is a FARM, not a beauty parlor!" He slammed the door and sat down and sulked. And while he sulked, it began to rain.

It poured down in barrel loads. The barnyard got lumpy, the paintwork got splattered, and the flowers got rained down flat.

"Oh no!" said Farmer Joe.
"There's going to be another dreadful letter!"
But then he had an idea.

He got a great big piece of paper and wrote on it in great big letters:

Dear Disgruntled,

If you don't like it, you can clean it up yourself.

Sincerely,
Farmer Joe

"Humph!" snorted Louisa.
"If that is the way it's going to be,
I shall go SOMEWHERE BETTER!"

She packed her things and hitched a ride to the city.

Farmer Joe watched Louisa go.
So THAT was Disgruntled!

"Yahoo!" cried Farmer Joe.
"No more annoying letters,
no more silly ideas, and
NO MORE Disgruntled!"

But . . .

The city was smoky and smoggy and smelly.
And Louisa wasn't pleased with it at all.

So she wrote another letter.

Dear Farmer Joe,

The city is all very well, but I think you must be missing me terribly.
Very truly yours,
Gruntled!
(also known as Louisa)
xxx

P.S. See you soon.

S   P

And the very next day
she set off . . .

. . . back to the farm.